Ollie's Ski Trip

Elsa Beskow

On Ollie's sixth birthday, his father gave him a pair of skis. He hadn't had *proper* skis before, just a pair that the foreman's son, John, had made for him out of bits of plank — so you can imagine how much he wanted to try them out.

But winter did not seem to want to come that year. Now and then, of course, it snowed a bit, but even before the ground was white all over, the snow melted again. So Ollie watched and waited and longed for winter and wondered, "Will it ever come this year?"

But in the end it did.

A week or two before Christmas, snow began falling in big flakes, and it went on for two whole days and nights without stopping. Everything was covered with a thick white blanket. And when Ollie woke on the third morning, the sky was shining blue and the snow sparkled like millions of stars.

Ollie was so excited, he went head over heels three  times on his bed without stopping. He scrambled into his clothes, not caring if they went on the right way round or not. Then he ran in to see his mother.

"Mum, Mum, can I go out *now*, this minute?"

"Listen," said his mother. "You must have some breakfast first. And don't forget your mittens, because it's cold today."

Ollie gulped down his porridge and milk. His mother helped him into his thick coat and long mittens, stuffed a sandwich into both pockets, and told him that he could stay out until dinner time. Then he waved goodbye to his mother and his little brother and, fastening on his new skis, he skied over the thick, white snow towards the forest.

The trees were so pretty! And as he went deeper into the forest, they looked even more wonderful. It was like going into an enchanted palace, and Ollie said to himself, "Thank you, King Winter. I'm so glad you came!"

The next moment he almost fell over backwards with surprise, for there in front of him stood an old man, glittering white from head to toe. Ollie stared at him. "Are you King Winter?" he asked.

"Oh no," said the old man. "I'm only Jack Frost. What do you think of the forest today?"

"Did you do it?" asked Ollie. "How did you make it all sparkle?"

"It's easy," said Jack Frost, and he breathed on Ollie's coat. His breath hung like a white cloud, and when it disappeared, Ollie's coat was covered with glistening hoar frost.

Then he laughed and gave Ollie's ear a little pinch. "You're a sharp lad," he said, "and I don't think you mind if the cold wind stings your face a bit. You called out King Winter's name a moment ago, so maybe you'd like to come with me to his palace here in the forest."

"Oh, yes please!" said Ollie excitedly. So off they went through the forest, Jack Frost first and Ollie following.

All of a sudden, Ollie began to sneeze. His feet felt wet and the hoar frost on his coat had melted. Just then, a strange old woman came stomping through the forest in big, black galoshes that squelched with every step. She had a broom over her shoulder and an umbrella in one hand, and she was blowing her nose and sneezing all the time as if she had a terrible cold.

Who was she?

Ollie was just going to ask her, when Jack Frost rushed forwards shouting, "What! You again? Go away at once and don't you dare stick your nose in here before spring!"

And then he blew a huge cloud at her. She looked quite scared and ran away so fast that she dropped her broom.

Ollie was so surprised, he couldn't think what to say. "You were very rude to that old woman," he said in the end.

"Oh, so I was rude, was I?" growled Jack Frost, still looking angry. "Well nothing makes me crosser than that woman, Mrs Thaw. Just look at the mess she's made here." And he pointed to the nearest tree, where the frost had already begun to melt. Then he went round breathing on everything and made it all as lovely as it had been before.

"A good thing she didn't have time to do much more damage," he said a little more cheerfully. "You see, Mrs Thaw is really Winter's cleaning lady, and she is supposed to clear up before Spring comes. But she's so stupid; she never knows when she is meant to come and even turns up with her slush in the middle of winter and wrecks everything. You only have to turn your back and there she is! Well, Ollie, shall I call her back?"

"No, don't do that!" said Ollie, horrified. "She doesn't have to come back, does she?"

"Oh, no. I've scared her away for a long time now," Jack Frost said, "but you can never be quite sure with her. I'd make the most of the snow, if I were you, and I'd use my skis every day. But now, we must hurry. It's not far to King Winter's palace."

Before long, they came to a huge castle. It was built of snow and guarded by two polar bears. The bears sniffed at Jack Frost like friendly dogs as he and Ollie walked through the gateway. Then the visitors went across a courtyard and through an iron-studded door made of polished ice.

They came into a huge room and at the far end, two walruses stood beside a throne of ice. There sat King Winter, and his calm face looked stern. For the first time, Ollie shivered and felt a little afraid.

But Jack Frost led him up to the throne. "This is a very nice boy, Your Majesty," he said. "A little while ago, he was so pleased that you have arrived that he was calling your name in the forest."

Then King Winter smiled, and his eyes gleamed like the northern lights.

"I'm glad to hear it," he said. "You do know how to ski, I suppose?"

"Oh, yes," said Ollie.

"And toboggan?"

"Yes. Head first and feet first and sideways, too!" said Ollie.

"And skate?"

"I haven't got any skates," said Ollie.

"No reason why you shouldn't have some," said King Winter. "But now that you're here, would you like to look round my palace?"

And he nodded to Ollie and Ollie bowed a very deep bow and followed Jack Frost into the next room.

The walls and the high, curved ceiling were made of hard-packed snow. A fire burned in the middle of the floor and the smoke went out through a hole in the roof. Round the fire sat little people, working away happily. The men were making ski boots and the women were knitting thick socks. They were so busy, they hardly had time to look up. Jack Frost didn't like the fire, so he hurried through the room quickly.

In the next room some girls were knitting ski-mitts
with long cuffs, and embroidering them with red roses.
They were very busy too, but they did have time to look
up at Ollie.

Then came the room that looked like a big workshop,
where some boys were building skis and toboggans and
sledges; while in one corner, others were making skate
blades. They all worked so fast and Ollie watched and
wished that he was as clever with his hands as they were.

"Why are you so busy?" Ollie asked one of the boys.

"Well, we've got to hurry now if we want to get
finished by Christmas," said the boy. "You see, everyone
wants their presents for Christmas. But we'll be going
out to play in a moment."

Just then, a gong sounded and all the children
streamed out, sweeping Ollie along with them.

And what a time he had! Everyone wanted to play with Ollie and he joined in with everything. First, they skied down a slope with big dips in it, then they taught Ollie to skate on the pond. Next they built snowmen and a big snowcastle that they all stormed, and soon there was a huge snow fight, with snowballs flying about in all directions.

Then they tied their toboggans together in a long line and slid down the slope, bumping over the dips. All of a sudden, there was a loud whistle and in a flash the children had disappeared back inside the palace, leaving Ollie standing by himself, panting and hot.

"Had a good time?" asked Jack Frost, appearing suddenly.

"Oh, yes!" said Ollie.

"That's good," said Jack Frost, with a pleased smile.

Then he harnessed a reindeer, stepped onto Ollie's skis, and with Ollie holding on behind him, they drove off. Jack Frost knew a shortcut home across the moor

where Ollie used to pick cloudberries in the summer.

At the edge of the trees, Jack Frost said goodbye. Ollie arrived home so full of what had happened that he could scarcely eat a thing.

And, would you believe it? On Christmas morning, Ollie heard a knock at his window. He tried to look out, but he couldn't see a thing because the glass was covered with the loveliest frost flowers. But he knew at once that Jack Frost had paid him a visit. He went out onto the porch, and there lay two parcels; one was for him and in it was a pair of magnificent skates. In the other, there was a toboggan for his little brother.

That winter, Ollie used his skis and skates nearly every day, because Mrs Thaw kept out of the way for longer than usual. Perhaps she was afraid of Jack Frost, or maybe it was because whenever it looked as though it was going to thaw, Ollie and his brother went outside and said:

"Mrs Thaw, Mrs Thaw,
Please don't sweep our snow away!
Come again another day!"

Whichever it was, she didn't come again all winter.

She didn't come until springtime, when King Winter and his court had moved up to the North Pole. Then she came with a splash. What a mess! Whatever Ollie said then didn't help, not even when his little brother pleaded:

"Dear Mrs Thaw, please go!
Don't take away our snow!"

She didn't stop until there wasn't a speck of snow left. Rain poured down in torrents and last year's withered leaves were sent whirling away by her broom. And everyone seemed to get a cold. Ollie was really angry with Mrs Thaw.

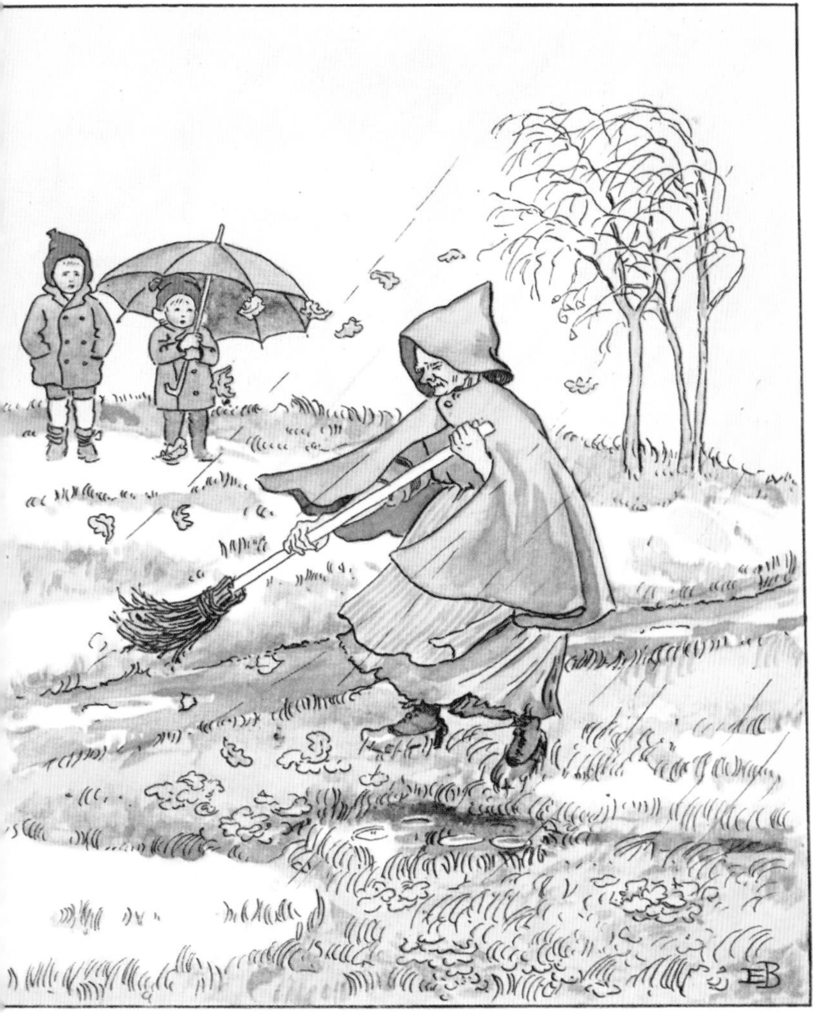

But one lovely spring day, Spring came driving up in her airy carriage drawn by white butterflies. Then Ollie saw Mrs Thaw, as she stood by the side of the ditch wearing a brand new apron. She curtsied to Spring, beaming with delight. For the first time, Ollie really liked Mrs Thaw, and knew that she wasn't so bad after all. But he did wish she would learn to come at the proper time.

First published in Swedish in 1907 as *Ollies Skidfärd*
First published in English in 1981
This edition published in 2008 by Floris Books
15 Harrison Gardens, Edinburgh www.florisbooks.co.uk
Fifth printing 2014
© 2007 BonnierCarlsen Förlag
English version © Ernest Benn Ltd, 1988
British Library CIP Data available
ISBN 978-086315-647-2
Printed in Malaysia